• THIS IN WHICH

• THIS IN WHICH

• BY GEORGE OPPEN

● NEW DIRECTIONS • SAN FRANCISCO REVIEW

For June

Who first welcomed
me home

CONTENTS

'Wait a minute,' Randall said insistently. 'Are you trying to describe the creation of the world—the universe?'

'What else?'

'But—damn it, this is preposterous! I asked for an explanation of the things that have just happened to *us*.'

'I told you that you would not like the explanation.'

—Robert A. Heinlein, The Unpleasant Profession
of Jonathan Hoag

'. . . the arduous path of appearance.'

—Martin Heidegger

- THIS IN WHICH

• TECHNOLOGIES

Tho in a sort of summer the hard buds blossom
Into feminine profusion

The 'inch-sized
Heart,' the little core of oneself,
So inartistic,

The inelegant heart
Which cannot grasp
The world
And makes art

Is small

Like a small hawk
Lighting disheveled on a window sill.

Like hawks we are at least not
Nowhere, and I would say
Where we are

Tho I distract
Windows that look out
On the business
Of the days

In streets
Without horizon, streets
And gardens

Of the feminine technologies
Of desire
And compassion which will clothe

Everyone, arriving
Out of uncivil
Air
Evil
As a hawk

From a hawk's
Nest as they say
The nest of such a bird

Must be, and continue
Therefore to talk about
Twig technologies

• ARMIES OF THE PLAIN

1

'A zero, a nothing':
Assassin.

Not nothing. At nineteen
Crossing frontiers,

Rifleman of the suffering—
Irremediable suffering—of the not-great,

Hero and anti hero
Of our time

Despite all he has cost us
And he may have cost us very much

2

Ruby's day,
Bloomsday.

Ruby

Proud to have learned survival
On the harsh plains — —

Bloomsday.

A man
'Of the Jewish faith . . .'

'and it is so stupid . .
And I never use the term . .'

Whose people wrote
Greatly

Desperate the not great,
Like Oswald the not great

Locked
In combat.

• PHILAI TE KOU PHILAI

There is a portrait by Eakins
Of the Intellectual, a man
Who might be a school teacher
Shown with the utmost seriousness, a masculine drama
In the hardness of his black shoes, in the glitter
Of his eyeglasses and his firm stance—
How have we altered! As Charles said
Rowing on the lake
In the woods, 'if this were the country,
The nation, if these were the routes through it—'

How firm the man is
In that picture
Tho pedagogic.
This was his world. Grass
Grows to the water's edge
In these woods, the brown earth
Shows through the thinned grass
At the little landing places of vacation

Like deserted stations,
Small embarkation points: We are
Lost in the childish
Here, and we address
Only each other
In the flat bottomed lake boat
Of boards. It is a lake
In a bend of the parkway, the breeze
Moves among the primitive toys
Of vacation, the circle of the visible

The animal looked across

And saw my eyes . . . Vacation's interlude?
When the animal ran? What entered the mind
When dawn lit the iron locomotives,
The iron bridges at the edge of the city,

Underpinnings, bare structure,
The animal's bare eyes

In the woods . . .
'The relation of the sun and the earth

Is not nothing! The sea in the morning'
And the hills brightening, Loved

And not loved, the unbearable impact
Of conviction and the beds of the defeated,

Children waking in the beds of the defeated
As the day breaks on the million

Windows and the grimed sills
Of a ruined ethic

Bursting with ourselves, and the myths
Have been murderous,

Most murderous, stake
And faggot. Where can it end? Loved, Loved

And Hated,
Rococo boulevards

Backed by the Roman
Whose fluted pillars

Blossoming antique acanthus

Stand on other coasts
Lifting their tremendous cornices.

• PSALM

Veritas sequitur . . .

In the small beauty of the forest
The wild deer bedding down—
That they are there!

                Their eyes
Effortless, the soft lips
Nuzzle and the alien small teeth
Tear at the grass

                The roots of it
Dangle from their mouths
Scattering earth in the strange woods.
They who are there.

                Their paths
Nibbled thru the fields, the leaves that shade them
Hang in the distances
Of sun

                The small nouns
Crying faith
In this in which the wild deer
Startle, and stare out.

These are the small resorts
Of the small poor,
The low sandspits
And the honkytonks
On the far side
Of the becalmed bay. The pennant
Flies from the flagstaff
Of the excursion steamer
Which carried us
In its old cabins
Crossing the bay
Tho it is flimsily built
And fantastic, its three white decks
Towering now above the pier
That extends from the beach
Into water barely deep enough
Over the sand bottom.

1

THE GESTURE

The question is: how does one hold an apple
Who likes apples

And how does one handle
Filth? The question is

How does one hold something
In the mind which he intends

To grasp and how does the salesman
Hold a bauble he intends

To sell? The question is
When will there not be a hundred

Poets who mistake that gesture
For a style.

THE LITTLE HOLE

The little hole in the eye
Williams called it, the little hole

Has exposed us naked
To the world

And will not close.

Blankly the world
Looks in

And we compose
Colors

And the sense

Of home
And there are those

In it so violent
And so alone

They cannot rest.

THAT LAND

Sing like a bird at the open
Sky, but no bird
Is a man—

Like the grip
Of the Roman hand
On his shoulder, the certainties

Of place
And of time

Held him, I think
With the pain and the casual horror
Of the iron and may have left
No hope of doubt

Whereas we have won doubt
From the iron itself

And hope in death. So that
If a man lived forever he would outlive
Hope. I imagine open sky

Over Gethsemane,
Surely it was this sky.

PAROUSIA

Impossible to doubt the world: it can be seen
And because it is irrevocable

It cannot be understood, and I believe that fact is lethal

And man may find his catastrophe,
His Millennium of obsession.

                              air moving,
a stone on a stone,
something balanced momentarily, in time might the lion

Lie down in the forest, less fierce
And solitary

Than the world, the walls
Of whose future may stand forever.

FROM VIRGIL

I, says the buzzard,
I—

Mind

Has evolved
Too long

If 'life is a search
For advantage.'

'At whose behest

Does the mind think?' Art
Also is not good

For us
Unless like the fool

Persisting
In his folly

It may rescue us
As only the true

Might rescue us, gathered
In the smallest corners

Of man's triumph. *Parve puer* . . . 'Begin,

O small boy,
To be born;

On whom his parents have not smiled

No god thinks worthy of his table,
No goddess of her bed'

Parked in the fields
All night
So many years ago,
We saw
A lake beside us
When the moon rose.
I remember

Leaving that ancient car
Together. I remember
Standing in the white grass
Beside it. We groped
Our way together
Downhill in the bright
Incredible light

Beginning to wonder
Whether it could be lake
Or fog
We saw, our heads
Ringing under the stars. We walked
To where it would have wet our feet
Had it been water

• GUEST ROOM

There is in age

The risk that the mind
Reach

Into homelessness, 'nowhere to return.' In age
The maxims

Expose themselves, the happy endings
That justify a moral. But this?

This? the noise of wealth,

The clamor of wealth—tree
So often shaken—it is the voice

Of Hell.
The virtue of the mind

Is that emotion

Which causes
To see. Virtue . . .

Virtue . . . ? The great house
With its servants,

The great utensiled
House

Of air conditioners, safe harbor

In which the heart sinks, closes
Now like a fortress

In daylight, setting its weight
Against the bare blank paper.

●　●

The purpose
Of their days.

And their nights?
Their evenings
And the candle light?

What could they mean by that?
Because the hard light dims

Outside, what ancient
Privilege? What gleaming
Mandate

From what past?

If one has only his ability

To arrange
Matters, to exert force,

To open a window,
To shut it—

To cause to be arranged—

Death which is a question

Of an intestine
Or a sinus drip

Looms as the horror
Which will arrive

When one is most without defenses,

The unspeakable
Defeat

Toward which they live
Embattled and despairing;

It is the courage of the rich

Who are an *avant garde*

Near the limits of life—Like theirs

My abilities
Are ridiculous:

To go perhaps unarmed
And unarmored, to return

Now to the old questions—

● ●

Of the dawn
Over Frisco
Lighting the large hills
And the very small coves
At their feet, and we
Perched in the dawn wind
Of that coast like leaves
Of the most recent weed—And yet the things

That happen! Signs,
Promises—we took it
As sign, as promise

Still for nothing wavered,
Nothing begged or was unreal, the thing
Happening, filling our eyesight
Out to the horizon—I remember the sky
And the moving sea.

- GIOVANNI'S *RAPE OF THE SABINE WOMEN*
  AT WILDENSTEIN'S

Showing the girl
On the shoulder of the warrior, calling

Behind her in the young body's triumph
With its despairing arms aloft

And the men violent,
being violent

In a strange village. The dust

Settles into village clarity
Among the villagers, a difficult

Song
Full of treason.

Sing?

To one's fellows?
To old men? in the villages,

The dwindling heritage
The heart will shrivel in

Sometime—But the statue!

Spiraling its drama
In the stair well

Of the gallery . . . Useless!
Useless! Thick witted,

Thick carpeted, exhilarated by the stylish
Or the opulent, the blind and deaf. There was the child

The girl was:

Seeking like a child the eyes
Of the animals

To promise
Everything that matters, shelter

From the winds

The winds that lie
In the mind,
The ruinous winds

'Powerless to affect
The intensity of what is'—

'It has been good to us,'
However. The nights

At sea, and what

We sailed in, the large
Loose sphere of it

Visible, the force in it
Moving the little boat.

Only that it changes! Perhaps one is himself
Beyond the heart, the center of the thing

And cannot praise it

As he would want to, with the light in it, feeling the long
        helplessness
Of those who will remain in it

And the losses. If this is treason
To the artists, make the most of it; one needs such faith,

Such faith in it
In the whole thing, more than I,
Or they, have had in songs.

• A LANGUAGE OF NEW YORK

1

A city of the corporations

Glassed
In dreams

And images—

And the pure joy
Of the mineral fact

Tho it is impenetrable

As the world, if it is matter

Is impenetrable.

2

Unable to begin
At the beginning, the fortunate
Find everything already here. They are shoppers,
Choosers, judges . . . And here the brutal
Is without issue, a dead end.

                     They develop
Argument in order to speak, they become
unreal, unreal, life loses
solidity, loses extent, baseball's their game
because baseball is not a game
but an argument and difference of opinion
makes the horse races. They are ghosts that endanger

One's soul. There is change
In an air
That smells stale, they will come to the end
Of an era
First of all peoples
And one may honorably keep
His distance
If he can.

3

I cannot even now
Altogether disengage myself
From those men

With whom I stood in emplacements, in mess tents,
In hospitals and sheds and hid in the gullies
Of blasted roads in a ruined country,

Among them many men
More capable than I—

Muykut and a sergeant
Named Healy,
That lieutenant also—

How forget that? How talk
Distantly of 'the People'?

Who are the people? that they are

That force within the walls
Of cities

Wherein the cars
Of mechanics
And executives

Echo like history
Down walled avenues
In which one cannot speak.

4

Possible
To use
Words provided one treat them
As enemies.
Not enemies—Ghosts
Which have run mad
In the subways
And of course the institutions
And the banks. If one captures them
One by one proceeding

Carefully they will restore
I hope to meaning
And to sense.

5

Which act is
Violence

And no one makes do with a future
Of rapid travel with diminishing noise
Less jolting
And fewer drafts. They await

War, and the news
Is war
As always

That the juices may flow in them
And the juices lie.

Great things have happened
On the earth and given it history, armies
And the ragged hordes moving and the passions
Of that death

But who escapes
Death?

Whether or not there is war, whether he has
Or has not opinions, and not only warriors,
Not only heroes

And not only victims, and they may have come to the end
Of all that, and if they have
They may have come to the end of it.

6

There can be a brick
In a brick wall
The eye picks

So quiet of a Sunday.
Here is the brick, it was waiting
Here when you were born,

Mary-Anne

7

Strange that the youngest people I know
Like Mary-Anne live in the most ancient buildings

Scattered about the city
In the dark rooms
Of the past—and the immigrants,

The black
Rectangular buildings
Of the immigrants.

They are the children of the middle class.

'The pure products of America—'

Investing
The ancient buildings
Jostle each other

In the half-forgotten, that ponderous business,
This Chinese wall.

Whitman: 'April 19, 1864

The capital grows upon one in time, especially as they have got the great figure on top of it now, and you can see it very well. It is a great bronze figure, the Genius of Liberty I suppose. It looks wonderful toward sundown. I love to go and look at it. The sun when it is nearly down shines on the headpiece and it dazzles and glistens like a big star; it looks quite

curious . . .'

- EROS

Show me also whether there is more to come than is past,
or the greater part has already gone by us.—Second Esdras

'and you too, old man, so we have heard,
Once . . .'
An old man's head, bulging
And worn

Almost into death.

The head grows from within
And is eroded.

Yet they come here too, the old,
Among the visitors, suffering
The rain

Here above Paris—

To the plaque of the ten thousand
Last men of the Commune
Shot at that wall

In the cemetery of Père-Lachaise, and the grave
Of Largo Caballero and the monuments to the Resistance—

A devoutness

Toward the future
Recorded in this city
Which taught my generation

Art
And the great paved places
Of the cities.

Maze

And wealth
Of heavy ancestry and the foreign rooms

Of structures

Closed by their roofs
And complete, a culture

Mined
From the ground . . .

As tho the powerful gift
Of their presence
And the great squares void
Of their dead

Were the human tongue
That will speak.

• BOY'S ROOM

A friend saw the rooms
Of Keats and Shelley
At the lake, and saw 'they were just
Boys' rooms' and was moved

By that. And indeed a poet's room
Is a boy's room
And I suppose that women know it.

Perhaps the unbeautiful banker
Is exciting to a woman, a man
Not a boy gasping
For breath over a girl's body.

- PENOBSCOT

Children of the early
Countryside

Talk on the back stoops
Of that locked room
Of their birth

Which they cannot remember

In these small stony worlds
In the ocean

Like a core
Of an antiquity

Non classic, anti-classic, not the ocean
But the flat
Water of the harbor
Touching the stone

They stood on—

I think we will not breach the world
These small worlds least
Of all with secret names

Or unexpected phrases—

Penobscot

Half deserted, has an air
Of northern age, the rocks and pines

And the inlets of the sea
Shining among the islands

And these innocent
People
In their carpentered

Homes, nailed
Against the weather—It is more primitive

Than I know
To live like this, to tinker
And to sleep

Near the birches
That shine in the moonlight

Distant
From the classic world—the north

Looks out from its rock
Bulging into the fields, wild flowers
Growing at its edges! It is a place its women

Love, which is the country's
Distinction—

The canoes in the forest
And the small prows of the fish boats
Off the coast in the dead of winter

That burns like a Tyger
In the night sky. One sees their homes and lawns,
The pale wood houses

And the pale green
Terraced lawns.
'It brightens up into the branches

And against the buildings'
Early. That was earlier.

• SEATED MAN

The man is old and—
Out of scale

Sitting in the rank grass. The fact is
It is not his world. Tho it holds

The machine which has so long sustained him,
The plumbing, sidewalks, the roads

And the objects
He has owned and remembers.
He thinks of murders and torture

In the German cellars
And the resistance of heroes

Picturing the concrete walls.

- STREET

Ah these are the poor,
These are the poor—

Bergen street.

Humiliation,
Hardship . . .

Nor are they very good to each other;
It is not that. I want

An end of poverty
As much as anyone

For the sake of intelligence,
'The conquest of existence'—

It has been said, and is true—

And this is real pain,
Moreover. It is terrible to see the children,

The righteous little girls;
So good, they expect to be so good . . .

• CARPENTER'S BOAT

The new wood as old as carpentry

Rounding the far buoy, wild
Steel fighting in the sea, carpenter,

Carpenter,
Carpenter and other things, the monstrous welded seams

Plunge and drip in the seas, carpenter,
Carpenter, how wild the planet is.

There are the feminine aspects,
The mode in which one lives
As tho the color of the air
Indoors
And not indoors

Only—. What distinction
I have is that I have lived
My adult life
With a beautiful woman, I have turned on the light
Sometimes, to see her

Sleeping—The girl who walked
Indian style—straight-toed—
With her blond hair
Thru the forests

Of Oregon
Has changed the aspect
Of things, everything is pierced
By her presence tho we have wanted
Not comforts

But vision
Whatever terrors
May have made us
Companion
To the earth, whatever terrors—

For love we all go
To that mountain
Of human flesh
Which exists
And is incapable
Of love and which we saw
In the image
Of a woman—We said once
She was beautiful for she was
Suffering
And beautiful. She was more ambitious
Than we knew
Of wealth
And more ruthless—speaking
Still in that image—we will never be free
Again from the knowledge
Of that hatred
And that huge contempt. Will she not rot
Without us and die
In childbed leaving
Monstrous issue—

• BAHAMAS

Where are we,
Mary, where are we?
They screen us and themselves
With tree lined lanes

And the gardens of hotels tho we have traveled
Into the affluent tropics. The harbors
Pierce all that. There are these islands

Breaking the surface
Of the sea. They are the sandy peaks
Of hills in an ocean

Streaked green by their shoals. The fishermen
And the crews from Haiti
Tide their wooden boats out

In the harbors. Not even the guitarists
Singing the island songs
To the diners

Tell of the Haitian boats
Which bear their masts, the tall
Stripped trunks of trees

(Perhaps a child
Barefoot on the ragged deck-load
Of coconuts and mats, leans

On the worn mast) across the miles
Of the Atlantic, and the blinding glitter
Of the sea.

• THE FOUNDER

Because he could not face
A whole day
From dawn

He lay late
As the privileged
Lie in bed.

Yet here as he planned
Is his village
Enduring

The astronomic light
That wakes a people
In the painful dawn.

• PRIMITIVE

A woman dreamed
In that *jacal,* a jungle hut, and awoke
Screaming in terror. The hut
Stands where the beach
Curves to a bay. Here the dug-out is hauled
Clear of the surf, and she awoke
In fear. Their possessions
Are in the hut and around it
On the clean ground under the trees: a length
       of palm trunk
Roughened by uses, a wash tub,
The delicate fish lines
His fingers know so well—
They were visible in the clear night. Here she awoke

Crying in nightmare
Of loss, calling her husband
And the baby woke also
Crying

- ALPINE

We were hiding
Somewhere in the Alps
In a barn among animals. We knew
Our daughter should not know
We were there. It was cold
Was the point of the dream
And the snow was falling

Which must be an old dream
Of families

Dispersing into adulthood
And the will cowers

In the given.

Eros—the will—
Eros!

That no thing
Shelters

• RATIONALITY

there is no 'cure'
Of it, a reversal
Of some wrong decision—merely

The length of time that has passed
And the accumulation of knowledge.

To say again: the massive heart
Of the present, the presence
Of the machine tools

In the factories, and the young workman
Elated among the men
Is homesick

In that instant
Of the shock
Of the press

In which the manufactured part

New in its oil
On the steel bed is caught
In the obstinate links

Of cause, like the earth tilting
To its famous Summers—that 'part

of consciousness'. . .

• NIGHT SCENE

The drunken man
On an old pier
In the Hudson River,

Tightening his throat, thrust his chin
Forward and the light
Caught his raised face,
His eyes still blind with drink . . .

Said, to my wife
And to me—
He must have been saying

Again—

Good bye Momma,
Good bye Poppa

On an old pier.

THE MAYAN GROUND

. . . and whether they are beautiful or not there will be
no one to guard them in the days to come . .

We mourned the red cardinal birds and the jeweled
*   ornaments*
And the handful of precious stones in our fields . . .

Poor savages
Of ghost and glitter. Merely rolling now

The tire leaves a mark
On the earth, a ridge in the ground

Crumbling at the edges
Which is terror, the unsightly

Silting sand of events—

Inside that shell, 'the speckled egg'
The poet wrote of that we try to break

Each day, the little grain,

Electron, beating
Without cause,

Dry grain, father

Of all our fathers
Hidden in the blazing shell

Of sunlight—. Savages,

● QUOTATIONS

1

When I asked the very old man
In the Bahamas
How old the village was
He said,
'I found it.'

2

The infants and the animals
And the insects
'stare at the open'

And she said
Therefore they are welcome.

3

'. . . and her closets!
No real clothes—just astounding earrings
And perfumes and bright scarves and dress-up things—

She said she was "afraid," she said she was
"always afraid." '

4

And the child
We took on a trip
Said

'We're having the life of our times'

5

Someone has scrawled
Under an advertisement in the subway
Showing a brassy blond young woman
With an elaborate head-dress:
'Cop's bitch.'

• RED HOOK: DECEMBER

We had not expected it, the whole street
Lit with the red, blue, green
And yellow of the Christmas lights
In the windows shining and blinking
Into distance down the cross streets.
The children are almost awed in the street
Putting out the trash paper
In the winking light. A man works
Patiently in his overcoat
With the little bulbs
Because the window is open
In December. The bells ring,

Ring electronically the New Year
Among the roofs
And one can be at peace
In this city on a shore
For the moment now
With wealth, the shining wealth.

• THE BICYCLES AND THE APEX

How we loved them
Once, these mechanisms;
We all did. Light
And miraculous,

They have gone stale, part
Of the platitude, the gadgets,
Part of the platitude
Of our discontent.

Van Gogh went hungry and what shoe salesman
Does not envy him now? Let us agree
Once and for all that neither the slums
Nor the tract houses

Represent the apex
Of the culture.
They are the barracks. Food

Produced, garbage disposed of,
Lotions sold, flat tires
Changed and tellers must handle money

Under supervision but it is a credit to no one
So that slums are made dangerous by the gangs
And suburbs by the John Birch Societies

But we loved them once,
The mechanisms. Light
And miraculous . . .

• THE OCCURRENCES

The simplest
Words say the grass blade
Hides the blaze
Of a sun
To throw a shadow
In which the bugs crawl
At the roots of the grass;

Father, father
Of fatherhood
Who haunts me, shivering
Man most naked
Of us all, O father

       watch
At the roots
Of the grass the creating
Now   that tremendous
plunge

• MONUMENT

Public silence indeed is nothing

So we confront the fact with stage craft
And the available poses

Of greatness,

One comes to the Norman chapel,
The Norman wall
Of the armed man
At the root of the thing,
Roughly armed,
The great sword, the great shield
And the helmet,
The horned helmet

On the mount
In the sea threatening
Its distances.

I was born to
A minor courage
And the harbor
We lived near, and the ungainliness
Of the merchants, my grandparents;

Of which I chose the harbor
And the sea

Which is a home and the homeless,
It is the sea,
Contrary of monuments
And illiberal.

• FLIGHT

Outside the porthole life, or what is
Not life streams in the air foils
Battering the wing tips, the houses
Small as in the skulls of birds, the frivolous ground

Of homes from which the force of motors
And the great riveted surfaces
Of the wings hold us, seated side by side
In flight, in the belly of force

Under the ceiling lights—the shabby bird
Of war, fear
And remoteness haunt it. We had made out
A highway, a city hall,

A park, but now the pastless ranches
Of the suburbs
Drift with the New World
Hills and the high regions

Which taken unaware
Resist, and the wings
Bend

In the open. Risk
And chance and event, pale
Ancestry beyond the portholes
Outside with the wings and the rivets.

• NIECE

The streets of San Francisco,
She said of herself, were my

Father and mother, speaking to the quiet guests
In the living room looking down the hills

To the bay. And we imagined her
Walking in the wooden past
Of the western city . . . her mother

Was not that city
But my elder sister. I remembered

The watchman at the beach
Telling us the war had ended—

That was the first world war
Half a century ago—my sister
Had a ribbon in her hair.

• THE ZULU GIRL

Her breasts
Naked, the soft
Small hollow in the flesh
Near the arm pit, the tendons
Presenting the gentle breasts
So boldly, tipped

With her intimate
Nerves

That touched, would touch her
Deeply—she stands
In the wild grasses.

The steel worker on the girder
Learned not to look down, and does his work
And there are words we have learned
Not to look at,
Not to look for substance
Below them. But we are on the verge
Of vertigo.

There are words that mean nothing
But there is something to mean.
Not a declaration which is truth
But a thing
Which is. It is the business of the poet
'To suffer the things of the world
And to speak them and himself out.'

O, the tree, growing from the sidewalk—
It has a little life, sprouting
Little green buds
Into the culture of the streets.
We look back
Three hundred years and see bare land.
And suffer vertigo.

- A NARRATIVE

1

I am the father of no country
And can lie.

But whether mendacity
Is really the best policy. And whether

One is not afraid
To lie.

2

And truth? O,
Truth!

Attack
On the innocent

If all we have
Is time.

3

The constant singing
Of the radios, and the art

Of colored lights
And the perfumist

Are also art. But here

Parallel lines do not meet
And the compass does not spin, this is the interval

In which they do not, and events
Emerge on the bow like an island, mussels

Clinging to its rocks from which kelp

Grows, grass
And the small trees

Above the tide line
And its lighthouse

Showing its whitewash in the daylight

In which things explain each other,
Not themselves.

4

An enclave
Filled with their own
Lives, they said, but they disperse

Into their jobs,
Their 'circles,' lose connection
With themselves . . . How shall they know

Themselves, bony
With age?
This is our home, the planets

Move in it
Or seem to,
It is our home. Wolves may hunt

With wolves, but we will lose
Humanity in the cities
And the suburbs, stores

And offices
In simple
Enterprise.

5

It is a place.
Nothing has entered it.
Nothing has left it.
People are born

From those who are there. How have I forgotten . .

How have we forgotten
That which is clear, we
Dwindle, but that I have forgotten
Tortures me.

6

I saw from the bus,
Walked in fact from the bus station to see again
The river and its rough machinery
On the sloping bank—I cannot know

Whether the weight of cause
Is in such a place as that, tho the depth of water
Pours and pours past Albany
From all its sources.

7

Serpent, Ouroboros
Whose tail is in his mouth: he is the root
Of evil,
This ring worm, the devil's
Doctrine the blind man
Knew. His mind
Is its own place;
He has no story. Digested

And digesting—Fool object,
Dingy medallion
In the gutter
Of Atlantic Avenue!
Let it alone! It is deadly.
What breath there is
In the rib cage we must draw
From the dimensions

Surrounding, whether or not we are lost
And choke on words.

8

But at night the park
She said, is horrible. And Bronk said
Perhaps the world
Is horror.
She did not understand. He meant
The waves or pellets
Are thrown from the process
Of the suns and like radar
Bounce where they strike. The eye
It happens
Registers
But it is dark.
It is the nature
Of the world:
It is as dark as radar.

9

     The lights
Shine, the fire
Glows in the fallacy
Of words. And one may cherish
Invention and the invented terms
We act on. But the park
Or the river at night
She said again
Is horrible.

10

Some of the young men
Have become aware of the Indian,
Perhaps because the young men move across the continent
Without wealth, moving one could say
On the bare ground. There one finds the Indian

Otherwise not found. Wood here and there
To make a village, a fish trap in a river,
The land pretty much as it was.

And because they also were a people in danger,
Because they feared also the thing might end,
I think of the Indian songs . . .
'There was no question what the old men were singing'
The anthropologist wrote,

Aware that the old men sang
On those prairies,
Return, the return of the sun.

11

River of our substance
Flowing
With the rest. River of the substance
Of the earth's curve, river of the substance
Of the sunrise, river of silt, of erosion, flowing
To no imaginable sea. But the mind rises

Into happiness, rising

Into what is there. I know of no other happiness
Nor have I ever witnessed it. . . . Islands
To the north

In polar mist
In the rather shallow sea—
Nothing more

But the sense
Of where we are

Who are most northerly. The marvel of the wave
Even here is its noise seething
In the world; I thought that even if there were nothing

The possibility of being would exist;
I thought I had encountered

Permanence; thought leaped on us in that sea
For in that sea we breathe the open
Miracle

Of place, and speak
If we would rescue
Love to the ice-lit

Upper World a substantial language
Of clarity, and of respect.

• PRO NOBIS

I believe my apprenticeship
In that it was long was honorable
Tho I had hoped to arrive
At an actuality
In the mere number of us
And record now
That I did not.

Therefore pray for us
In the hour of our death indeed.

● FROM A LETTER TO C T

One imagines himself
addressing his peers
I suppose. Surely
that might be the definition
of 'seriousness'? I would like,
as you see,
to convince
myself
that my pleasure in your response
is not
plain vanity
but the pleasure of being heard,
the pleasure
of companionship, which seems
more honorable.

- WORLD, WORLD—

Failure, worse failure, nothing seen
From prominence,
Too much seen in the ditch.

Those who will not look
Tho they feel on their skins
Are not pierced;

One cannot count them
Tho they are present.

It is entirely wild, wildest
Where there is traffic
And populace.

'Thought leaps on us' because we are here. That is the fact
        of the matter.
Soul-searchings, these prescriptions,

Are a medical faddism, an attempt to escape,
To lose oneself in the mystical self.

The self is no mystery, the mystery is
That there is something for us to stand on.

We want to be here.

The act of being, the act of being
More than oneself.

George Oppen was born in 1908 in New Rochelle, New York. He is married and has one daughter. He and his wife live in Brooklyn, New York. He is the author of two previous books: *Discrete Series,* published in 1934 by the Objectivist Press, and *The Materials,* published in 1962 by New Directions / San Francisco Review (ND Paperbook 122).

● Other New Directions/San Francisco Review Poetry